R0083475137

08/2015

Curious George®

Plays Mini Golf

Adaptation by Marcy Goldberg Sacks
Based on the TV series teleplay
written by Craig Miller

Houghton Mifflin Company
Boston

For information about permission to reproduce selections from this book, write to
Permissions, Houghton Mifflin Company, 215 Park Avenue South, New York, New York 10003.

Library of Congress Cataloging-in-Publication Data is on file.

Design by Afsoon Razavi and Marcy Goldberg Sacks

www.hmhco.com

Printed in China
SCP 10 9 8
4500501773

George and Steve were good friends.
They liked to play games.
Steve always had the high score.
He always won.

One day Steve invited George to
play mini golf.
This was a new game for George.
He was curious.
Maybe he could win this time.

Steve hit the ball one . . . two . . .
three times.
Now it was George's turn.

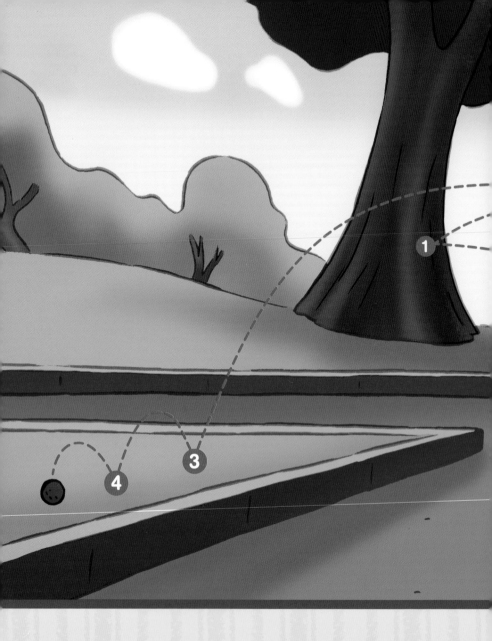

George took a big swing.
His ball hit two trees!

George swung his golf club
many times to get a high score.

George hit the ball again and
again and again.

It went all over the golf course.
Golf was easy!

George hit the ball as many times
as he could.
Finally, he hit it right into the hole.

At the end of the game, Steve read
the scores:
Steve, 35, Betsy, 58, and George . . .
250!

George had the highest score.
He was so happy.
He had won.

"But George, in golf the *lowest*
score is best," Betsy told him.
"I won the game," Steve said.

George was surprised.
How could a small number be
better than a big number?

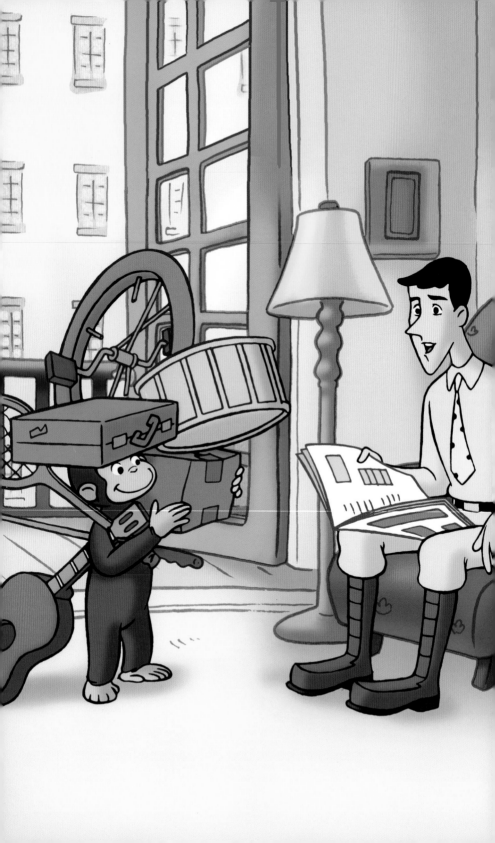

George had an idea.
He wanted to win in golf.
He had to practice.
George asked his friend if he
could borrow some things from
their house.

George made a golf course on the roo
A paper towel roll was his club.
He blew in one end.
Air came out the other end.

The ball moved.
He was ready to play.
George invited Steve over.

George played first.
He blew through the tube . . . and go
a hole in one!

Steve was next.
But it took him eight tries to get
the ball into the hole.

Steve counted the points.
George had the lowest score.
Finally he was the winner — of
monkey mini golf!